# THE KING'S
# GIFT

For John
     *(K.L.)*
For John Siow
     *(D.K.)*

Produced by Martin International Pty Ltd
Published in association with Era Publications,
220 Grange Road, Flinders Park, South Australia 5025

Text © Kath Lock, 1995
Illustrations © David Kennett, 1995
Cover design by Steven Woolman
Printed in Hong Kong
First published 1995

**National Library of Australia
Cataloguing-in-Publication Data:**
Lock, Kath, 1943-
     The king's gift.

     ISBN 1 86374 072 4.
     ISBN 1 86374 081 3 (pbk.).

     I. Kennett, David, 1959-     . II. Title.

A823.3

Available in:

**Australia** from Era Publications, 220 Grange Road,
Flinders Park, South Australia 5025

**Canada** from Vanwell Publishing Ltd, 1 Northrup Cresc.,
PO Box 2131, Stn B, St Catharines, ONT L2M 6P5

**New Zealand** from Reed Publishing, 39 Rawene Road,
Birkenhead, Auckland 10

**Singapore, Malaysia & Brunei** from
Publishers Marketing Services Pte Ltd, 10-C Jalan Ampas,
#07-01 Ho Seng Lee Flatted Warehouse, Singapore 1232

**United Kingdom** (Hardcover) from Ragged Bears Ltd,
Ragged Appleshaw, Andover, Hampshire SP11 9HX;
(Paperback) from Heinemann Educational Publishers,
Halley Court, Jordan Hill, Oxford OX2 8EJ

# THE KING'S
# GIFT

Written by Kath Lock

Illustrated by David Kennett

ong ago and far away there were two brothers who had served together in the army for many years. All their lives the two brothers had been quite different from each other. One was kind, gentle and hard-working, while the other was lazy, harsh and dishonest.

When they were babies, one had been easy to feed and care for; the other was naughty and constantly defiant.

As they grew to be young men, one was kind to his parents and fellows. He worked in the fields for long hours, and he was always willing to be of service to the townsfolk. His brother, alas, was lazy, and spent his time gambling and fighting.

The folk who lived in the town where the two brothers lived had often wondered why it should be that they were so very different.

And so it was when they went into the army. Their fellow workers were amazed that the two could be brothers, for one was honest and diligent while the other constantly brought shame on his troop.

For all of the years that the brothers were in the army their comrades and officers wondered about them. Had they not had the same parents, and been raised in the same town and surroundings? What could it be that made them as they were? Why was it that one was kind-hearted and hard-working, yet the other was a rogue during work and play?

Eventually, when the brothers left the army, it was the dishonest brother who was wealthy, and the virtuous brother who was poor.

The rich brother built himself an elegant house and lived in an extravagant manner, caring nothing for the costs incurred by his lavish entertainments and excessive lifestyle. He made his money by gambling with his equally greedy friends and by taking advantage of those around him.

All his poor brother could afford was a rented hut and a small over-worked plot of land which, in spite of his diligence, produced crops of a poor quality. He could barely earn enough money to survive. In spite of his poverty he was happy; and he was liked and respected by all who knew him.

One night there was a terrible storm. An old woman who happened to be travelling through the district went to the house of the rich brother. From a distance she had seen the lights and heard the music and merriment within. She begged for food and shelter for the night. The wealthy brother refused her and sent her on her way immediately. As she left, she heard him and his friends laugh at her unhappy plight.

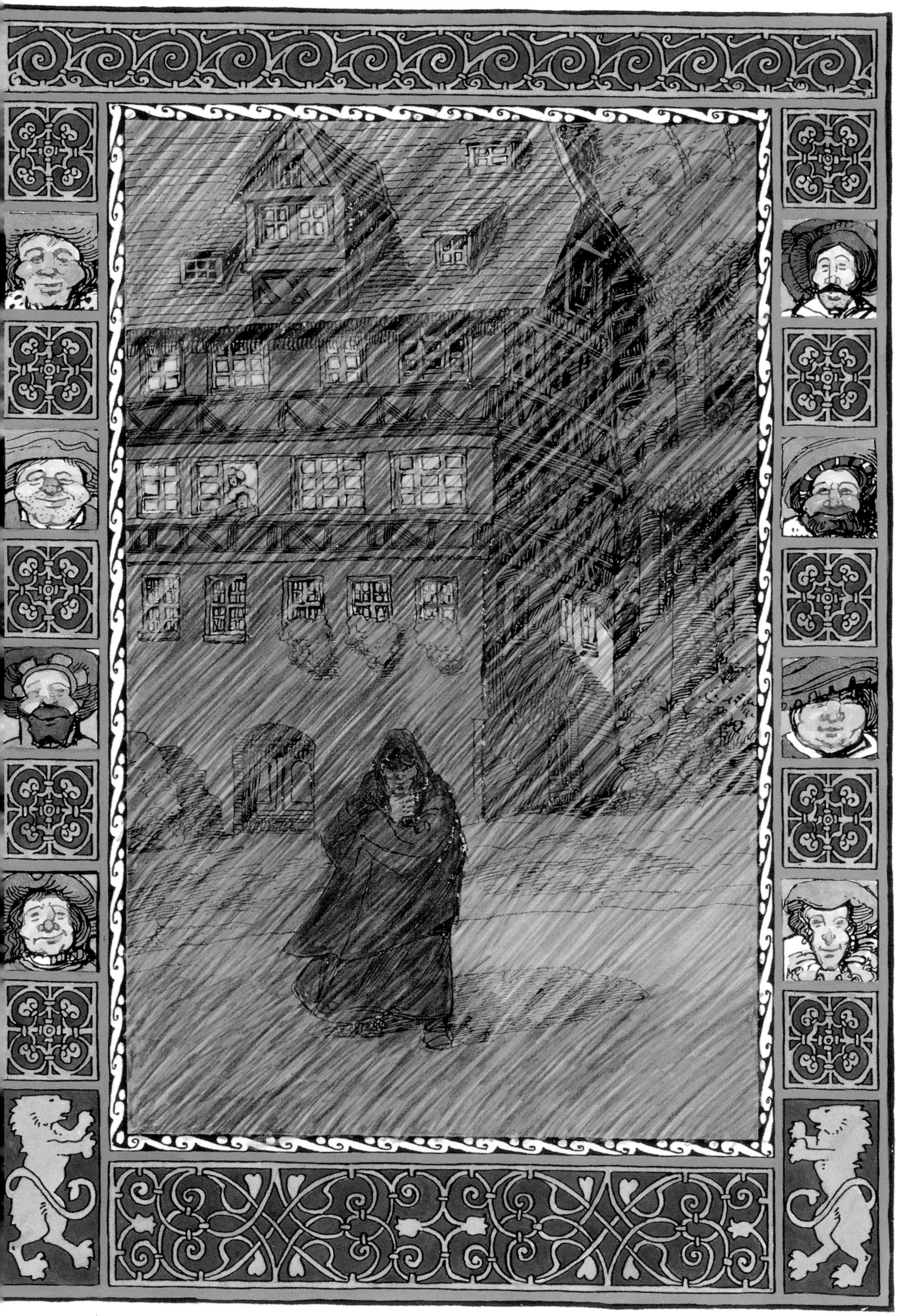

She soon came to the hut of the poor brother, who willingly welcomed her into his dry shelter and shared with her the small amount of food which he had. He prepared a sleeping place for her by the fire, and gave her his meagre supply of blankets to keep her warm through the night.

The following morning, as she was leaving, she pointed to the poor brother's over-worked field.

"Plant turnips," she said and she walked away.

When the planting season arrived the poor brother remembered what the old woman had said. He turned the soil as best he could with his meagre tools, and he sowed the whole field with turnip seed.

It was not long before the turnip crop was growing well. However, in the middle of the field was one turnip which was quite extra-ordinary. In just a few weeks it had grown as big as a melon. When the other turnips stopped growing this turnip continued, yet clearly it was not ready for harvesting. Long after the other turnips had been harvested and sold, the giant turnip was still growing.

The poor brother didn't know what to do with it.

"Who would want to buy such a giant turnip?" he asked his friends.

"Take it to the castle. This surely is the king of turnips. Perhaps our king will buy it from you?"

So the poor brother waited until the turnip was ready, harvested it with the help of the townsfolk, and loaded it into his cart. He borrowed donkeys from his friends, and then drove the cart to the king.

The king was amazed.

"What a giant turnip!" he exclaimed. "Never before have I seen such a magnificent specimen."

He called his wife the queen, their children and all of the courtiers to see the turnip.

They were all amazed to see such an enormous vegetable. No one had seen anything like it before.

"How does it happen that you are able to grow such a wonderful vegetable?" asked the queen. "Do you have magic powers?"

"Alas, no," said the poor brother. "I am a simple farmer who rents a small field in your kingdom. My brother is wealthy and has much land, but I have nothing to distinguish me."

"Aha!" said the king. "We shall change that."

He bought the turnip, paying the poor brother handsomely with land, cattle, money and jewels, for he considered the turnip to be of great value. He ordered that the turnip be displayed where all who visited the castle would be able to see it and marvel at its wonder.

Now that the king had rewarded him, the brother who had been poor was even more wealthy than his rich brother.

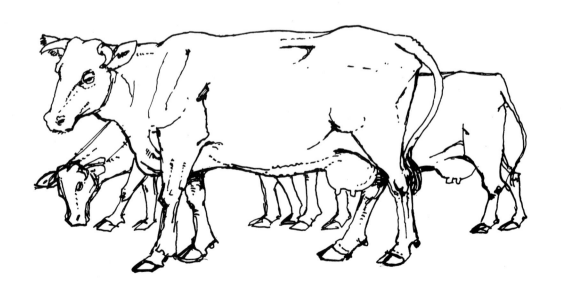

It was not long before the selfish brother heard people talking about the extraordinary gift which his brother had given to the king and about how the king had rewarded his brother just for having given him a turnip.

At first he was furious that such a thing could happen. Almost immediately he began to spend all of his time wondering how he could impress the king and become even richer than he already was.

Eventually he devised a plan.

He harnessed all of his horses to his biggest cart, and he filled the cart with his lavish possessions — gold, silver, jewels, silks and furniture. Everything he owned that was of value was put onto the cart.

Then he took the cart to the king, asking himself all along the way: if the king would exchange wealth for an old turnip, then what would he give in return for all of these riches?

Again the king was amazed.

The rich brother humbled himself and crawled before the king and his courtiers. He promised fealty forever as he handed his possessions to the king and queen.

Eagerly, he awaited their response to his generous gift.

"What can we give in return?" asked the king of his wife. "Such faithfulness should be well rewarded. What can we give that such a wealthy man does not already have?"

Then the king thought of the perfect gift for someone who has everything.

He presented the brother with the giant turnip.